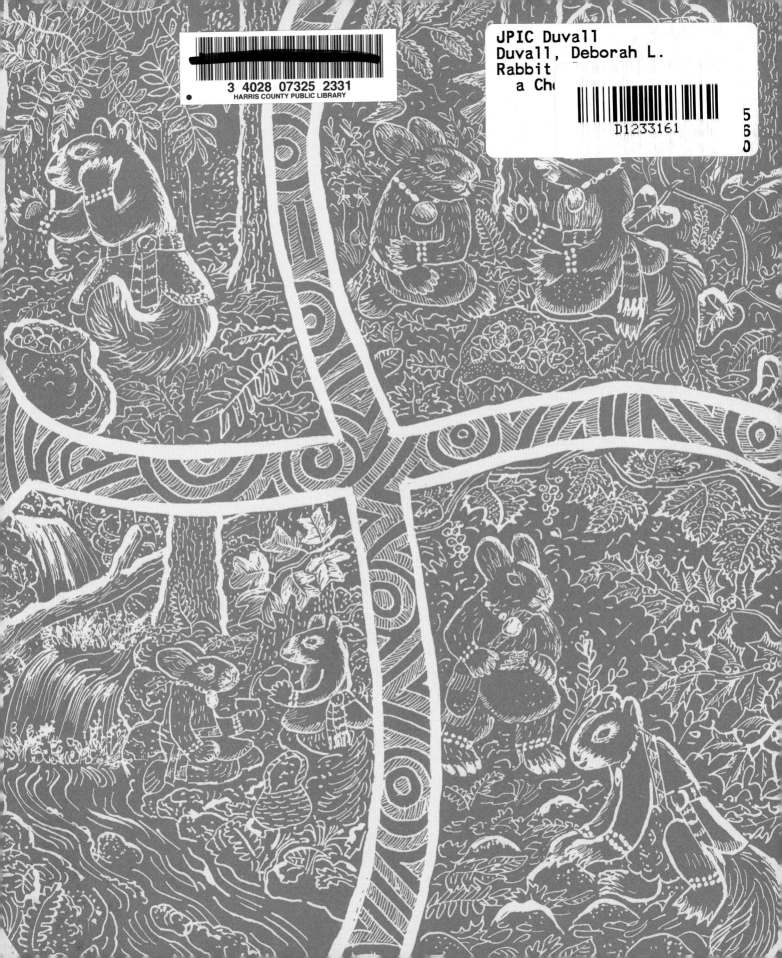

RABBIT PLANTS THE FOREST

RABBIT PLANTS THE FOREST

A CHEROKEE WORLD STORY

STORY BY DEBORAH L. DUVALL

PAINTINGS BY MURV JACOB

University of New Mexico Press ❦ Albuquerque

FOR WALT KELLY, WHO BROUGHT US POGO,
"WE HAVE MET THE ENEMY, AND HE IS US."

ARTIST'S NOTES: The renowned Cherokee painter and traditionalist Cecil Dick once told me, "Most of the ancient Cherokees never hunted squirrels because the squirrels plant the forest." That bit of wisdom passed on is the inspiration for Duvall's story. *Rabbit Plants the Forest* is a contemporary story based on the Animals in traditional Cherokee tales.

Although now deeply embellished with more recent Appalachian legends, we believe the stories about the Wampus Cat are of ancient Cherokee origin. These stories are popular and still evolving in the southeastern United States. Wampus Cat stories appear to have been used for many generations to scare young children so they don't go too far into the forest. It should be remembered that five hundred years ago, the entire eastern United States area was one contiguous forest. Contemporary personal appearances by the Wampus Cat, however, seem to be mostly limited to mascots at the occasional high school sporting event.

—M. Jacob

© 2006 by the University of New Mexico Press
All rights reserved. Published 2006

11   10   09   08   07   06   1   2   3   4   5   6   7

Library of Congress Cataloging-in-Publication Data

Duvall, Deborah L., 1952–
  Rabbit plants the forest / Deborah Duvall, Murv Jacob.
     p. cm.
  ISBN-13: 978-0-8263-3691-0 (cloth : alk. paper)
  ISBN-10: 0-8263-3691-4 (cloth : alk. paper)
  1. Cherokee Indians—Folklore. 2. Rabbit (Legendary character)
I. Jacob, Murv, ill. II. Title.
  E99.C5D897 2006
  398.2'089'97557—dc22
                                        2005020761

Design by Melissa Tandysh
Printed and bound in Singapore by Tien Wah Press

Rabbit, whose Cherokee name is Ji-Stu …

…left his house in the broom grass meadow before the morning light and scampered down the forest path. The other animals elected Ji-Stu as "the Messenger" because he could travel faster than most anyone. As he followed the path to the river, he came to the home of Otter, who lived in a burrow hidden beneath the hollow of a huge oak tree. Outside, Otter was busy cooking breakfast. He called Ji-Stu over to show off the morning's catch of fish.

"Oh, Ji-Stu," Otter said as Ji-Stu turned to go, "today is a good day for planting. Take that message to Sa-lo-li the Squirrel and I will cook lunch for you tomorrow."

"How do you know that today is good?" Ji-Stu demanded.

"That, my friend, is a secret!" Otter laughed. "Maybe Sa-lo-li will tell you."

Ji-Stu sped toward the squirrel's home in the forest. Sa-lo-li the Squirrel was famous. She knew the secrets of the trees and how they grew. Since the world was new, her family had planted the great oaks and hickories. And Sa-lo-li loved to talk. Yes, Ji-Stu would learn Otter's secret soon enough.

"Si-yo, Ji-Stu, hello down there!" Sa-lo-li popped her head through the door of her leafy nest as Ji-Stu called up to her. In seconds, she landed on the ground beside him. "I hope you have a message for me today!"

"I will tell you in a moment," Ji-Stu replied. "But first, what a strange house you have, Sa-lo-li! How did you build such a house?"

"I wove my house like a fine basket, with vines and leaves and twigs, strong enough to withstand the winter wind. Inside, my house is lined with warm fur and bright feathers." As she spoke, Sa-lo-li's tail twitched around in every direction.

Ji-Stu craned his head upward. He wanted to see the house for himself, but he had never climbed so high before. Even more, Ji-Stu wanted to know how Otter knew that today was a good day to plant.

"Now what is my message, Ji-Stu?" Sa-lo-li interrupted his thoughts.

"I will tell you in a moment, but first you must answer another question," Ji-Stu said. "How does Otter know that today is a good day to plant?"

"That, my friend, is a secret!" Sa-lo-li's words were the same as Otter's. "But you just told me the message, Ji-Stu. Today is planting day!"

Ji-Stu watched sadly as Sa-lo-li almost flew up the oak tree and into her house. He could hear her moving things around inside and clucking loudly to herself. Ji-Stu had missed his only chance to learn Otter's secret, and he was feeling sorry for himself. He sighed as Sa-lo-li reappeared with a lumpy bag tied around her waist, carrying a basket of food.

"Well, I see you are still here, Ji-Stu the Messenger," Sa-lo-li fixed her shiny black eyes on him for a long moment; then she winked at him. "Would you like to help me with the planting?"

Ji-Stu raced to join Sa-lo-li as she jumped lightly across fallen limbs and patches of leaves. She ran from tree to tree, measuring the distance between their trunks. Finally she chose a spot in the center of a clump of trees where sunlight fell on the ground. There Sa-lo-li began to dig with her tiny front legs. When the hole was as deep as she could reach, she leaned back and beamed at Ji-Stu.

"Now it is your turn," Sa-lo-li grinned.

She pointed to a sunny spot a few feet away. Ji-Stu giggled to himself. If a tiny squirrel could dig a hole that quickly, a strong rabbit could dig one twice as fast. He strode to the spot and scratched at the ground with one paw. But when he looked down, the ground was just the same as before. He scratched again, harder, but when he looked down, there was no hole. Sa-lo-li shooed Ji-Stu away from the spot and dug a perfect hole immediately.

"Maybe you can help me prepare the seeds, Ji-Stu," she said as she untied the lumpy bag around her waist.

Sa-lo-li emptied the contents of her bag before Ji-Stu. At once he recognized the smooth, tan hickory nuts, the long brown pecans, his favorite black walnuts, and all shapes and sizes of acorns.

"Those are not seeds!" Ji-Stu exclaimed. "You brought me walnuts for lunch. Thank you, Sa-lo-li!"

"Silly Ji-Stu!" Sa-lo-li teased. "Of course they are seeds! Hickory trees grow from hickory nuts, and oak trees grow from acorns, and walnut trees grow from walnuts! But to make them grow, you must crack their hard shells, like this ..."

Taking a hickory nut, Sa-lo-li opened her jaws wide and placed it between her sharp teeth. As she bit down, a perfect crack ran down its side.

Ji-Stu jumped up to catch the hickory nut Sa-lo-li pitched to him. Smiling, he opened his mouth and bit down. His teeth barely made a dent in the hard shell. He tried again and again, but the shell refused to crack. He gave up finally, shaking his head in disgust.

"Do not worry, Ji-Stu. There is still plenty of work for you to do," Sa-lo-li said as she grabbed the hickory nut, bit into its shell, and began rubbing the shell on her face.

"Sa-lo-li, is there something wrong with your face?" Ji-Stu's curiosity had overcome his disappointment. "Why are you doing that?"

"For the smell, Ji-Stu!" Sa-lo-li grinned proudly. "It is magic! The smell from my face stays on the hickory nut. Once it is planted, I will be able to find it again, even beneath the deepest snow."

Sa-lo-li quickly cracked and rubbed the pile of seeds, returning all but the hickory nuts to her bag. Then she dug new holes as Ji-Stu followed, dropping a hickory nut into each one and covering it with dirt. Ji-Stu made sure the soil was pressed firmly over the seeds by stomping it down with his big feet.

Once the hickories were in the ground, they hurried down to the riverside to plant Ji-Stu's favorite walnuts. Before long they saw a familiar face up ahead. It belonged to a tiny squirrel, white-haired and old. He stood outside the heavy door of his house in the hollow base of a huge tree. He leaned upon a fine walking stick, and he called to Ji-Stu.

"Si-yo, Ji-Stu the Messenger. Have you brought a message for me?"

"Oh, not today, White Oak." Ji-Stu raised his shoulders proudly. "I am here to plant walnuts!"

Everyone believed that White Oak reached his great old age by eating only bread made from white oak acorns. His neighbors gave him that name long ago, for both the acorns and his hair. Now he peered up at Ji-Stu.

"You may have no message for me, but I have one for you. While you plant your walnuts, keep one eye open for the Wampus Cat!" White Oak pointed to a huge track at Ji-Stu's feet.

Ji-Stu the Rabbit had traveled over miles and miles of this forest and never had he seen such a track. Yet still it seemed familiar. In fact, his friend Wildcat left tracks precisely like this one, only much, much smaller. Ji-Stu knew that White Oak the Squirrel enjoyed playing tricks almost as much as he did. He must be playing a trick now.

"You dug this track, White Oak!" said Ji-Stu. "Your artwork is good! It really does look like a giant cat stepped here."

"The Wampus Cat has two long, sharp teeth. The teeth look like flint knives and they hang way down below its jaws. Watch out for the Wampus Cat!" White Oak turned and disappeared into his tree.

"Don't be afraid, Ji-Stu," Sa-lo-li assured him when she saw his frightened face. "Old White Oak dug that cat track just like you said … it's only a silly trick!"

Ji-Stu quickly forgot White Oak's warning when he discovered how easily he could dig in the soft river bottom dirt. He dug almost as many holes as Sa-lo-li. Then Sa-lo-li took the walnuts from her pack and told Ji-Stu that he could plant them all! As he worked, he dreamed about the day when his walnut trees would grow tall, and he would be as famous as Sa-lo-li.

Ji-Stu worked until the sun was high in the sky. Then Sa-lo-li called for him to follow her. They stopped beside a splashing creek and ate a delicious lunch of bean bread and roseberry tea.

"Tell me more about the Wampus Cat," Ji-Stu said as Sa-lo-li filled his cup.

"Well, once my mother told me that the Wampus Cat comes from a country far from here, a country of giants." Sa-lo-li laughed and twitched her tail. "Those old squirrels, they like to try and fool you."

"Oh, and the Wampus Cat will try to catch you and eat you up!" Sa-lo-li continued to giggle as she spoke. "It hunts big animals by foot, and for smaller animals, like us, it leaves snares made of creeper vine."

"Then we had better watch where we step!" Ji-Stu sang, and both howled with laughter.

While Ji-Stu planted live oak acorns, Sa-lo-li went off in search of just the right place to start a grove of pecans. Now that he was alone, Ji-Stu let his grin stretch from ear to ear. So far as he knew, no one had ever been allowed to help Sa-lo-li on planting day. How jealous all his neighbors would be!

His grin became a look of alarm a moment later as a huge deer with wide antlers came charging past him. Then Ji-Stu heard a horrible roar from the direction the deer had come. He jumped behind a tree just as the Wampus Cat sailed in front of it!

Ji-Stu stared in disbelief as the huge creature slipped into the trees chasing the deer. He had glimpsed the awful teeth, hanging down like knives, just as White Oak had said. The eyes were full of yellow fire and the claws tore through the earth.

Ji-Stu's feet seemed rooted to the ground. He should have listened to White Oak. He should never have stayed to plant the walnuts with Sa-lo-li. Suddenly Ji-Stu remembered Sa-lo-li, alone in the woods! He must warn her about the Wampus Cat!

Ji-Stu ran in the direction Sa-lo-li had gone, listening intently, his heart beating like a dance drum. Then he heard a strange sound. It was a happy, tinkling sound, like chimes made of clamshell. Ji-Stu had always wanted a set of such chimes. Maybe their owner had seen Sa-lo-li.

He followed the sound and soon heard an outraged chattering just ahead. Ji-Stu's eyes bulged when he saw Sa-lo-li, hanging from a tree limb, her foot caught securely in a creeper vine snare.

"White Oak was telling the truth, Ji-Stu," Sa-lo-li wailed. "Oh, what if the Wampus Cat finds me!"

The thought of that made Sa-lo-li kick her legs wildly in the air, but the creeper vine snare held fast. As she kicked, Ji-Stu heard that sound of chimes again, coming from overhead this time. Looking up, he saw a set of clamshell chimes tied to the creeper vine above the struggling Sa-lo-li. Then he remembered seeing Otter use such a set of chimes on his fishing pole. The chimes alerted Otter each time a fish took his bait.

"Sa-lo-li, do not move!" Ji-Stu whispered urgently. "The Wampus Cat will know you are up there if it hears those chimes!"

Sa-lo-li froze in place, and Ji-Stu looked frantically toward the trees as they heard a loud roar. The Wampus Cat was coming, and it was coming fast! Somehow Ji-Stu must reach Sa-lo-li first. Quickly, he grabbed the rope-like stem of the creeper vine. If he climbed that vine to the top, he could chew through it and set Sa-lo-li free.

Up Ji-Stu climbed, high into the tree. He chewed through the vine easily, and in seconds Sa-lo-li dropped to the ground and ran, pulling the chimes behind her. Ji-Stu slid quickly down to follow, but it was too late. The Wampus Cat had seen them!

Ji-Stu and Sa-lo-li tore through the woods as fast as the wind. But the Wampus Cat ran faster! It was right on their heels when suddenly they saw old White Oak just ahead, yelling and waving them inside his hollow tree. The Wampus Cat slammed into the tree trunk just as Sa-lo-li and Ji-Stu ran through the little doorway. They heard it growling painfully as it limped away.

When he was sure the Wampus Cat had gone, Ji-Stu said goodbye to Sa-lo-li and made his way back to his little house in the broom grass meadow. Outside his house, Ji-Stu hung the clamshell chimes from Sa-lo-li's creeper vine snare. She said they would remind him to listen to the wisdom of old ones offering advice.

The next day, as promised, Otter arrived early to cook Ji-Stu his lunch. While Otter stirred the soup, Ji-Stu bragged about his new friendship with Sa-lo-li and how she had invited him to help her plant the forest again next year. Then he told Otter all about saving Sa-lo-li from the Wampus Cat. But still, he wanted to know Otter's secret.

"Please, Otter, you must tell me," Ji-Stu begged. "How did you know that yesterday was a good day to plant?"

"Oh, the Wampus Cat told me." Otter rolled his eyes and shook his head. "You can not fool me, Ji-Stu. The Wampus Cat is nothing but a story told by the old ones to scare us."

Just then Ji-Stu's clamshell chimes began to tinkle as a cool breeze swept across the broom grass meadow. He chuckled to himself, then filled his favorite bowl. And Otter's soup that day was the best Ji-Stu ever tasted!

Illustrations of Plants and Birds

Note: The round holes in the limestone rock beside the river were used by Cherokees to leach tannic acid from acorns used for food.

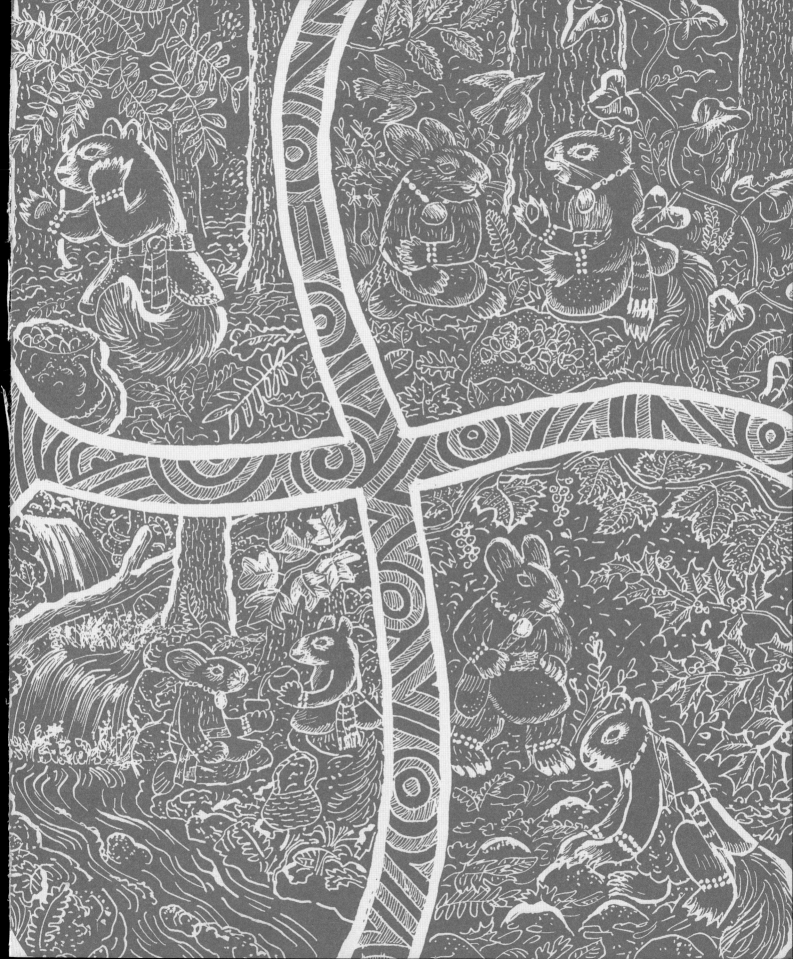